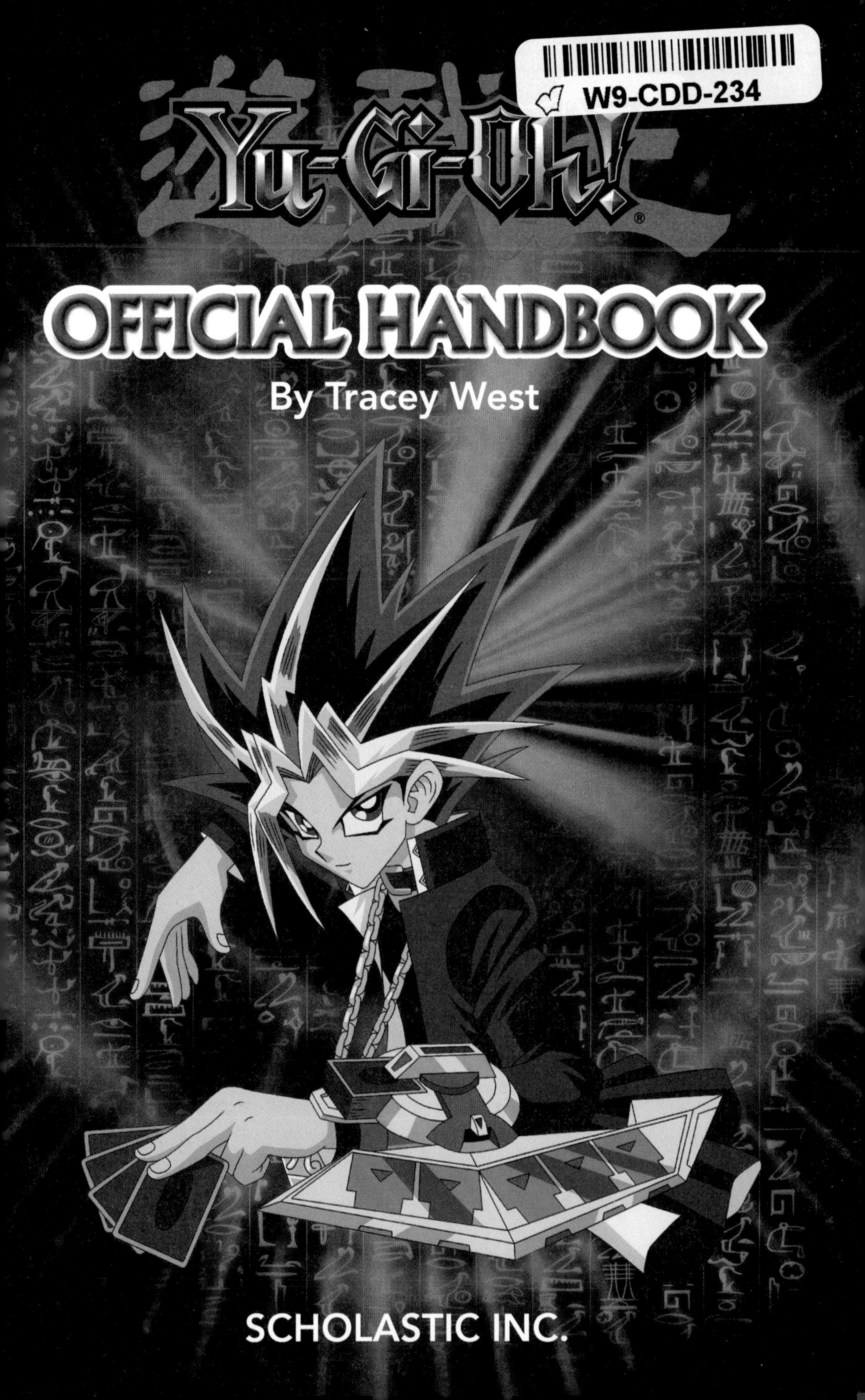

Yu-Gi-Oh!®
OFFICIAL HANDBOOK
By Tracey West
SCHOLASTIC INC.

Published by Scholastic Inc. under license from 4K Media.

Published by Scholastic Inc., *Publishers since 1920*. SCHOLASTIC and associated logos are trademarks and/or registered trademarks of Scholastic Inc.

ISBN 978-0-545-94075-7

12 11 10 9 8 7 6 5 4 3 2 1 16 17 18 19 20
Printed in the U.S.A. 40
First printing 2016

CONTENTS

WELCOME TO THE WORLD OF YU-GI-OH!

Monsters clash in the heat of battle.

Duelists face off against each other.

An ancient magic threatens to plunge the world into darkness.

Welcome to the world of Yu-Gi-Oh!, where duelists play a game with roots in ancient Egypt. Our hero is young Yugi Muto, who began his journey in hopes of becoming the best duelist he could be—and ended up saving the world.

Yugi's journey was full of ups and downs. He made new friends—and new enemies. He won battles, and lost battles. He discoverd how to duel with some of the most powerful Duel Monsters ever created. He learned of his connection to ancient Egypt. And through it all, he stayed loyal to the people closest to him.

This book is filled with everything you need to know about Yugi and the world of Duel Monsters. You'll meet Yugi's friends and foes. You'll read stories of amazing battles. And you'll get a closer look at the monsters who are the heart of this ancient game.

So what are you waiting for?

It's time to duel!

THE HISTORY OF DUEL MONSTERS

If you wish to become the best duelist you can be, then you must learn the dark and mysterious history of the game known as Duel Monsters. It began thousands of years ago, in ancient Egypt.

In ancient times, games were not played just for fun as they are today. People such as princes and pharaohs waged dueling games for power. These games were epic battles.

Egyptian sorcerers summoned monsters—real monsters—from within their souls and also from stone tablets. They made these monsters do their bidding. But as certain people used this power to do good, others used it to do evil. These Shadow Games brought Earth to the brink of destruction.

The citizens turned to the Pharaoh and his guardians for help. Using seven powerful magical objects known as the Millennium Items, he pulled the monsters out of people's hearts and sealed them away in stone tablets.

Five thousand years later, Maximillion Pegasus received one of the magical items, the Millennium Eye. He reinvented the game for modern times, using cards instead of real monsters.

Today, the ancient battles are being fought once more. When you, duelist, use your cards, you are reliving the past.

Use them wisely!

—Ishizu Ishtar

YU-GI-OH! DUEL MONSTERS TIMELINE

- Eons ago, the all-powerful Zorc emerged from the Shadow Realm.
- Years later, evil sorcerers learned how to summon monsters to play the Shadow Games.
- Aknadin, the brother of Pharaoh Aknamkanon, discovered a way to use the Millennium Spell Book to create the seven Millennium Items. With them, he told his brother, they could protect the kingdom from armies attacking Egypt. Pharaoh Aknamkanon agreed, never knowing that Aknadin had called upon the darkest of energies to create the Millennium Items, which released the great evil Zorc.

The Millennium Puzzle

- Pharaoh Aknamkanon learned of the destruction caused in order to create the Millennium Items. He asked the Egyptian gods for forgiveness and asked them to guide his son, Atem. When he died, Atem took his place.

- Bandit King Bakura attacked Pharaoh Atem and his guardians so he could get the Millennium Items.

- The key to sealing Zorc back in the Shadow Realm was the Pharaoh's real name. But Pharaoh knew that if anyone were to learn his real name, he or she could use it to release Zorc again. So he erased his own memories, locked his soul inside the Millennium Puzzle, and sealed away the Millennium Items.

- Years later, Grandpa Muto found the Millennium Puzzle.

- Shadi, the guardian of the Millennium Items, identified Maximillion Pegasus as the destined keeper of the Millennium Eye and gave it to him. When Pegasus visited Egypt, he learned about the Shadow Games and became curious about their magical powers. He created the game "Duel Monsters."

Maximillion Pegasus

- After eight years of trying, Yugi Muto put together the Millennium Puzzle Grandpa Muto had given him. He released Pharaoh's spirit, and it took refuge inside Yugi.
- Pegasus held the Duelist Kingdom Tournament. He hoped to defeat Seto Kaiba—a skilled duelist and head of KaibaCorp—so he could merge the Millennium Items with KaibaCorp technology to revive his lost love.
- In the final battle of the Duelist Kingdom tournament, Yugi defeated Pegasus.
- Shadi entered Yugi's mind, and Yugi learned of the Millennium Items. Soon after, Yami Yugi discovered that he was a powerful Pharaoh who had saved the world five thousand years ago.

Yugi Muto

- Ishizu Ishtar told Kaiba that he had links to ancient Egypt, and informed him about the three Egyptian God Cards. She gave Kaiba the Obelisk the Tormentor card, and told him the other two cards were in the hands of the Rare Hunters.
- Kaiba invented the Duel Disks, which were used for the first time in his Battle City tournament.
- Marik and his Rare Hunters challenged Yugi and his friends, who were searching for the Egyptian God Cards.

Seto Kaiba

- Marik entered the Battle City tournament, sending Odion in his place to battle Joey. But Marik's true identity was revealed—along with his sinister intentions.

- Yugi and his friends traveled by blimp to KaibaCorp Island to compete in the final rounds of the Battle City tournament. But Noah, a mysterious boy trapped in a virtual world, hijacked the blimp and brought Yugi and his friends inside his world.

- Yugi learned that Kaiba was really Noah's adopted brother. Years before, Noah's father, Gozaburo Kaiba, placed him in the virtual world. Yugi defeated Noah, and everyone escaped.

- In the Battle City finals, Yugi defeated Marik—winning the tournament and saving the world.

Marik

- A new villain emerged—Dartz, the ruler of the lost kingdom of Atlantis. Ten thousand years before, his kingdom was destroyed. Dartz sought to revive a powerful beast called the Grand Dragon Leviathan to destroy Earth so Atlantis could rise again. He and his followers began collecting souls with a card called The Seal of Orichalcos.

- Dartz and his henchmen won duels and collected souls. Atlantis rose from the ocean, and Yugi and Kaiba battled Dartz. Dartz gave up his own soul to resurrect the Grand Dragon Leviathan—but that terrible beast was no match for the Egyptian God Cards.

Dartz

- The KC Grand Championship began, pitting sixteen of the world's great duelists against each other.

- Yugi faced Leon von Schroeder in the Grand Championship finals—and won another tournament!

- Yami Yugi traveled back in time to regain his memories and learn about his past. He didn't realize that Bakura had lured him into the ultimate Shadow Game. The evil duelist wanted to re-create the past so that he could resurrect Zorc, the mighty creature of darkness.

Bakura

- Yugi, Joey, Tristan, Téa, and the spirit of Shadi traveled back in time to help Pharaoh. Kaiba later joined them.

- Bakura obtained the seven Millennium Items and found a way to resurrect Zorc without learning Pharaoh's secret name. Now only that name could send Zorc back to the darkness. Yugi, Tristan, and Joey discovered the Pharaoh's name, but they couldn't read the hieroglyphics. Before they could give the Pharaoh the name, Bakura challenged Yugi to a duel.

- Pharaoh's guardians battled Zorc and fell one by one. Only Guardian Seto escaped by going to the Shadow Realm.

- With the help of his friends, Yugi defeated Bakura. Pharaoh learned his true name, Atem, and once again defeated Zorc.

- Yugi and Pharaoh saved the world. But then the two had to compete in a ritual to decide their destiny—and to see if Yugi was ready to stand on his own. Yugi won, and Atem was free to leave Yugi and return to his fallen friends in the afterlife.

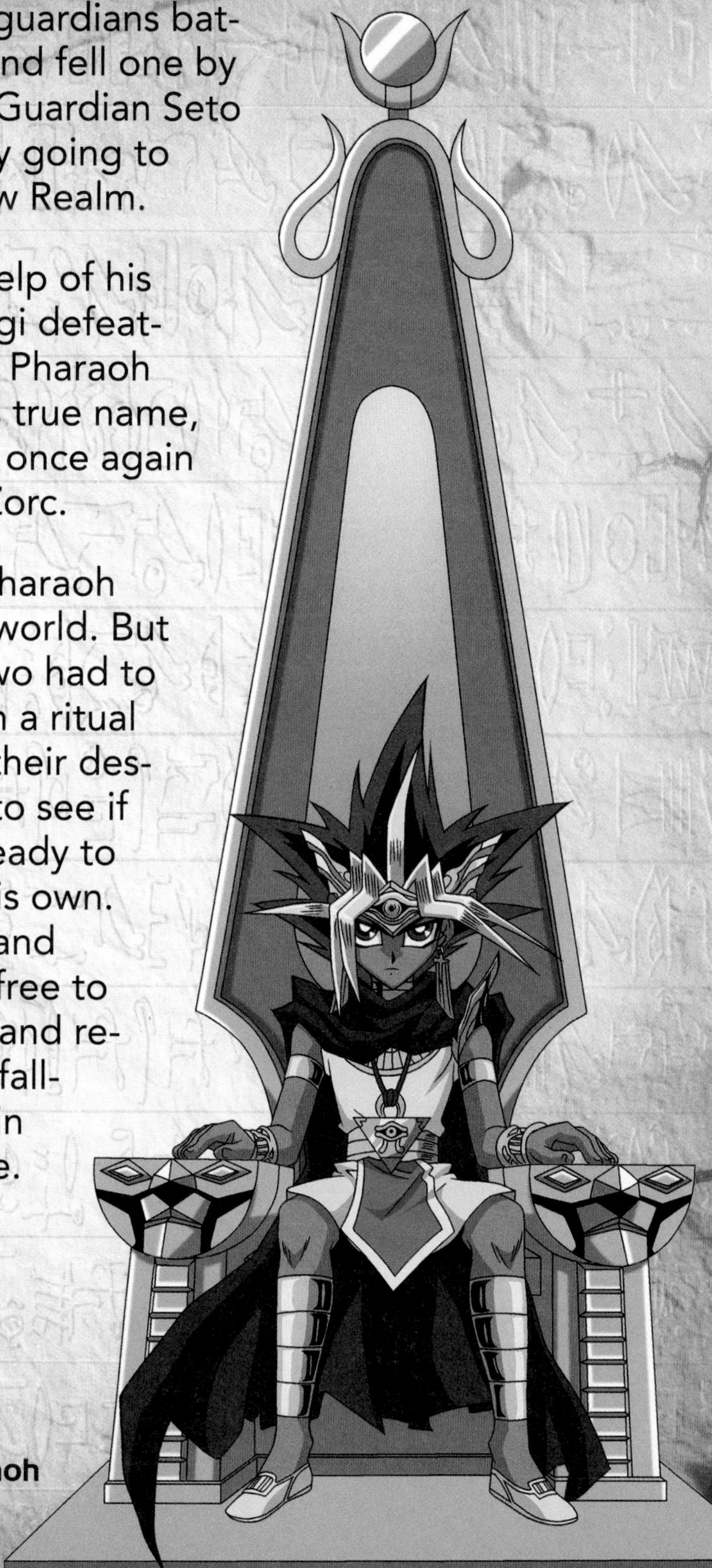

The Pharaoh

THE MILLENNIUM ITEMS

Created thousands of years ago in ancient Egypt and forged from dark energies, the Millennium Items can give special powers to the duelists who use them. For centuries, a mysterious Egyptian named Shadi guarded them.

"Each Millennium Item awaits the day it possesses those who claim it. Those who fail are punished."

—Shadi

Millennium Eye

Pegasus used this item to see the cards in his opponent's hand—and sometimes, to steal his opponent's soul! The Eye gives the bearer the ability to read his opponent's mind.

Millennium Key

When the Millennium Key is activated, you can enter another person's soul.

Millennium Necklace

With the necklace, Ishizu Ishtar could see into the future.

Millennium Puzzle

Inside this puzzle hides the greatest prize: Pharaoh's soul.

Millennium Ring

This Ring can detect the location of the other Millennium Items. It also allows the bearer to put his or her soul into other objects.

Millennium Rod

With the Millennium Rod, Marik could control the minds of his opponents.

Millennium Scale

The Millennium Scale allows the bearer to weigh the truth in a person's soul, allowing him or her to judge a person's crimes.

MAJOR CHARACTERS

Who is this spiky-haired kid, Yugi Muto, and why is he so important? What does it mean when he transforms into Yami Yugi? Who are Yugi's friends? Who are his enemies? Which duelists are the ones to watch out for, and which are easy to beat?

Read on to answer all these questions—and more! You'll also meet the major monsters used by each duelist.

"Believe in the heart of the cards!"

—Yugi

YUGI MUTO

Yugi began his journey as a freshman at Domino High School. His grandfather, Solomon Muto, taught him to play Duel Monsters. Grandpa taught Yugi about the heart of the cards, and showed him how to play with honor as well as skill.

Yugi started dueling his friends and classmates. Then one day, Grandpa gave Yugi an ancient artifact called the Millennium Puzzle. According to legend, whoever solved the puzzle would be granted dark and mysterious powers. The object captivated young Yugi.

It took Yugi many failed attempts, but he eventually solved the Millennium Puzzle! Then something amazing happened. The puzzle instilled Yugi with the spirit of an ancient Egyptian Pharaoh.

Pharaoh's powerful spirit helped Yugi gain strength and confidence—which made Yugi a better duelist. When he defeated master duelist Seto Kaiba, Yugi caught the attention of Maximillion Pegasus, the creator of the modern Duel Monsters game. That's when his adventure truly began.

Did You Know?

Yugi was destined to solve the Millennium Puzzle.

"Yugi, this looks dangerous. Let me take over!"

—Yami Yugi

YAMI YUGI

When Yugi lets the spirit of the ancient Pharaoh inside him, he becomes Yami Yugi. A master duelist, Yami Yugi is confident and skilled—and a fierce opponent. Yet he will never cheat, and always battles with honor.

With the help of Yami Yugi, young Yugi slowly but surely built his own confidence and self-esteem. But Yami Yugi learned something from Yugi, too—kindness, sympathy, and heart.

The link between Yugi and Yami Yugi is the Millennium Puzzle. The ancient Pharaoh sealed his soul inside it as a way to protect the world from the Shadow Games. And when the Shadow Games returned, and a powerful evil threatened the world, Yugi battled bravely on the front lines. But he couldn't do it alone—he couldn't have done it without Yami.

Did You Know?

- Yami Yugi is often called "The Pharaoh" by Yugi and his friends.
- In order to save the world, Pharaoh needed to learn his true name—Atem.

YUGI'S BIG MOMENTS

Yugi Defeats Pegasus

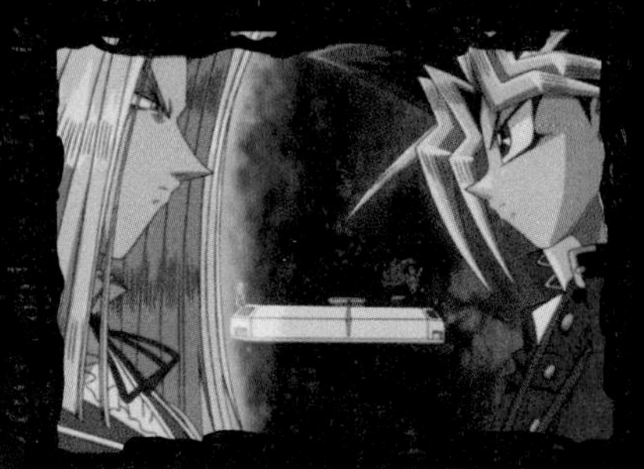

For Yugi, there was more at stake in winning the Duelist Kingdom tournament than just a championship title. Using his Millennium Eye, Pegasus had captured the souls of Grandpa, Mokuba, and Kaiba, and winning was the only way Yugi could get them back. Pegasus ensnared Yugi in a Shadow Game, nearly destroying Yugi. But Yugi's spirit survived, and he and Yami Yugi worked together to defeat Pegasus.

Yami Yugi Defeats Yami Marik in the Battle City Finals

Yugi entered the Battle City tournament and the pressure was on. In the final battle, Yami Yugi faced Yami Marik. The souls of Yugi and the good side of Marik were at stake. If Yami Yugi won, Yugi would be lost forever. In the end, Marik's good side took over Yami Marik. He surrendered the duel to Yami Yugi, saving Yugi.

Yami Yugi Recovers His Lost Memories

When Yugi and his friends traveled to Cairo, Egypt, they reunited with Ishizu, Marik, and Odion. They brought Yami Yugi to an ancient sanctuary containing the Tablet of Lost Memories. Yami Yugi was swept back in time to ancient Egypt, where he found himself reliving the ancient battle between good and evil. As the legendary chosen king, he was the only one who could call on the powers of the Egyptian God Monsters.

Yugi vs. Bakura in Ancient Egypt

Bakura resurrected Zorc, and the only thing that could stop him was Pharaoh's secret name. While Pharaoh battled Zorc, Bakura challenged Yugi to a duel to keep him from helping Pharaoh. Yugi used amazing strategy, but so did Bakura. At the end of the duel, Yugi had only one card left in his deck. He ummoned Gandora the Dragon of Destruction to wipe out all of Bakua's monsters. Then Silent Swordsman returned to decimate Bakura's life oints.

Pharaoh vs. Zorc

When Yugi and his friends gave Pharaoh his true name, ie finally had the key to deeating Zorc. First, he summoned the three Egyptian God Cards. Then he used Pharaoh's name to combine hem to form Holactie the Creator of Light. This ulra-powerful being banished Zorc forever.

A Duel for Destiny

With Zorc destroyed, Pharaoh's destiny was fulfilled, and he could now exist outside of Yugi. He could go on to the afterlife. But that would mean leaving Yugi all alone, and Pharaoh wasn't sure his best friend was ready for that. So he and Yugi fought a duel to decide his destiny. Yugi won the duel, and Pharaoh returned to the afterlife to rejoin his friends.

YUGI'S MONSTERS

Yugi has a host of fierce and diverse monsters—some more powerful than others. But the true strength of Yugi's monster collection doesn't lie in the monsters themselves, but in how he plays them.

Alpha The Magnet Warrior

Type: Rock

This monster uses magnetic power to attack its enemies. And because magnets attract each other, it can be combined with other Magnet Warriors.

B. Skull Dragon

Type: Dragon

What do you get when you merge Red-Eyes B. Dragon with Summoned Skull? This ferocious, powerful monster!

Beast of Gilfer

Type: Fiend

This dark, frightening creature can fly across the field on its leathery wings and swipe at enemies with its claws and tail.

Beaver Warrior

Type: Beast-Warrior

Don't underestimate this rodent fighter. Its spiked armor provides good defense, and it knows how to use his sword.

YUGI'S MONSTERS

Berfomet

Type: Fiend

How does a flying monster with four arms grab you? Any way it wants!

Beta The Magnet Warrior

Type: Rock

Magnet Warriors work best together, so bring Beta out onto the field with Alpha The Magnet Warrior.

Big Shield Gardna

Type: Warrior

He may not have a strong attack, but his defense . . . let's just say they don't call him "Big Shield" for nothing!

Black Luster Soldier

Type: Warrior

Spectators are amazed by the swordsmanship of this ferocious yet elegant knight.

Buster Blader

Type: Warrior

It takes a powerful warrior to wield a sword bigger than itself!

Catapult Turtle

Type: Aqua

This turtle's tough shell comes equipped with a catapult. It can destroy enemies with each shot fired.

YUGI'S MONSTERS

Celtic Guardian

Type: Warrior

A steadfast soldier, the Guardian will march bravely out onto the battlefield.

Chimera the Flying Mythical Beast

Type: Beast

This creature keeps its opponents guessing with attacks coming from one of its two heads—or from the hissing snake's head on the end of its tail!

Curse of Dragon

Type: Dragon

This wicked-looking dragon may get its powers from dark forces, but it has been known to save the day.

Dark Magician

Type: Spellcaster

This magician casts powerful spells over his enemies, and has a strong connection to Pharaoh in ancient Egypt.

Dark Magician Girl

Type: Spellcaster

Her spells are not to be taken lightly. She has trained with the best—Dark Magician.

YUGI'S MONSTERS

Dark Sage

Type: Spellcaster

The most powerful magician of all, he studied his craft for thousands of years.

Exodia the Forbidden One

Type: Dragon

Exodia is the guardian god for the ancient Egyptian palace. This card has helped Yugi defeat Kaiba. Some believe Exodia is just as powerful as the Egyptian God Cards.

Feral Imp

Type: Fiend

This creature might be playful, but when it enters the battlefield, look out!

Gaia the Dragon Champion

Type: Dragon

When Gaia The Fierce Knight rides Curse of Dragon, their combined powers are tough to beat.

YUGI'S MONSTERS

Gaia The Fierce Knight

Type: Warrior

Riding his trusty steed, Gaia needs no shield as he battles with two powerful lances!

Gamma The Magnet Warrior

Type: Rock

Gamma The Magnet Warrior fights with fury!

Gandora The Dragon of Destruction

Type: Dragon

When Yugi calls on this powerful card, the effects are truly destructive!

Giant Soldier of Stone

Type: Rock

This mountain of a monster battles with tons of raw power and fury—literally!

Green Gadget

Type: Machine

This monster is one mean, green fighting machine!

Holactie The Creator of Light

You must have all three Egyptian God Cards—Slifer the Sky Dragon, Obelisk the Tormentor, and The Winged Dragon of Ra—to summon this card.

YUGI'S MONSTERS

Horn Imp

Type: Fiend

Who needs a sword or a staff when you've got a wicked horn growing out of your forehead?

Jack's Knight

Type: Warrior

This knight in shining armor fights with bravery and honor.

King's Knight

Type: Warrior

With his massive muscles, King's Knight is a powerful opponent.

Kuriboh

Type: Fiend

This monster is very special to Yugi, and has a gentle and fun-loving personality. Kuriboh might not have strong attack or defense points, but it has special abilities that have helped lead Yugi to victory.

YUGI'S MONSTERS

Magician of Black Chaos

Type: Spellcaster

Monsters everywhere fear this powerful magician. Any way it wants!

Mammoth Graveyard

Type: Dinosaur

You won't find this monster in any dusty museum! It charges at opponents with its long, sharp tusks.

Marshmallon

Type: Fairy

"Is that a monster or a dessert topping?" asked Yami Bakura when Yugi played this monster. But Yugi had the last laugh. When you attack Marshmallon, you lose one thousand life points!

Mystical Elf

Type: Spellcaster

Peaceful by nature, this creature defends much better than she attacks.

Queen's Knight

Type: Warrior

With her gleaming sword and shield, Queen's Knight can hold her own—just like Jack's Knight and King's Knight.

Red Gadget

Type: Machine

Your opponents will see red when you bring this mechanical monster into battle!

YUGI'S MONSTERS

Silent Swordsman

Type: Warrior

Silent Swordsman can evolve to become stronger. He silences spells cast against him.

Silver Fang

Type: Beast

No collar or leash can restrain this ferocious canine!

Slifer the Sky Dragon

Type: Divine-Beast

Slifer the Sky Dragon is one of the legendary Egyptian God Monsters. The endless power of this divine dragon brings most monsters to their knees!

Egyptian God Card!

Stronghold the Moving Fortress

Type: Trap Monster

If you've got Red Gadget, Green Gadget, and Yellow Gadget, you can call on this card. The three Gadgets work together like gears to get Stronghold moving.

YUGI'S MONSTERS

Summoned Skull

Type: Fiend

With its green glowing eyes, large wings, and wicked horns, this powerful monster will strike terror into the hearts of your opponents.

Timaeus

Type: Dragon

An ancient protector of Atlantis, Timaeus was once a human, but he was transformed into a dragon. Yugi drew a sword, releasing the dragon from its crystal prison.

Legendary Guardian of Atlantis!

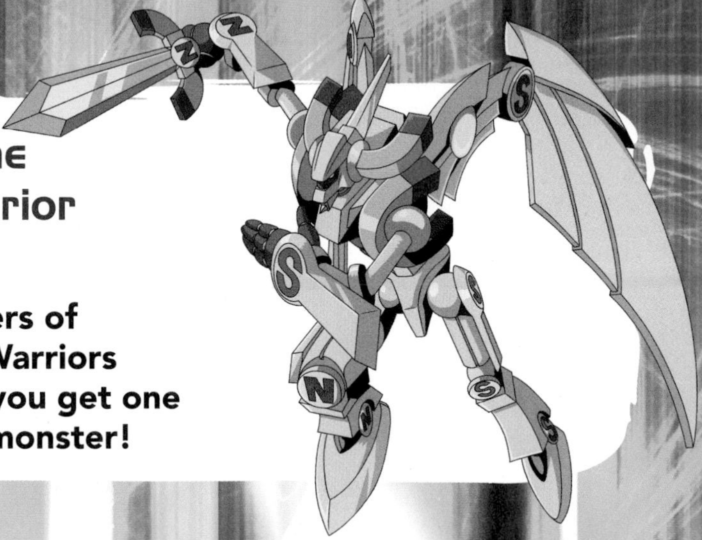

Valkyrion the Magna Warrior

Type: Rock

When the powers of three Magnet Warriors are combined, you get one very powerful monster!

Winged Dragon, Guardian of the Fortress #1

Type: Dragon

This magician casts powerful spells over his enemies, and has a strong connection to Pharaoh in ancient Egypt.

Yellow Gadget

Type: Machine

The third gadget monster packs a powerful mechanical punch!

YUGI'S FRIENDS AND FAMILY

JOEY WHEELER

Joey and Yugi met at Domino High School, and Joey quickly became his most loyal companion. Joey would do anything for his friends, but the person he cares for most in the world is his younger sister, Serenity.

His harsh street background means that Joey can be hotheaded sometimes, which can hurt him when he's dueling. But he's still hard to beat, and has risen in the ranks to become one of the world's top duelists.

Did You Know?

- Once, when Joey was bullying Yugi, he took a piece of Yugi's Millennium Puzzle from him and tossed it into a swimming pool! (He got it back for Yugi later.)
- Joey took lessons from Yugi's grandpa to become a better duelist.

SERENITY WHEELER

Joey and his younger sister were separated at a young age when their parents got divorced, yet they never forgot each other. When Serenity got sick, Joey battled in Duelist Kingdom Tournament to earn money for her eye operation. He didn't win, but Yugi gave him his winnings, and Serenity was cured. After that, Serenity often traveled with the duelists to cheer on her friends and help them in any way she could.

JOEY'S BIG MOMENTS

Joey Wins His First Tournament Duel

Joey had always dreamed of being a great duelist, and with Grandpa Muto's help, he really improved his skills. When he entered the Duelist Kingdom tournament, he found himself in a battle against veteran duelist Mai Valentine. If he had lost, he would have been out of the tournament. But with the help of Yugi and the support of his friends, he beat Mai to win his first tournament duel.

Joey Wins Red-Eyes B. Dragon

In the Duelist Kingdom tournament, Joey faced off against Rex Raptor and his dangerous dinosaur monsters. They rampaged all over Joey's monsters. Then Rex unleashed his secret weapon, Red-Eyes B. Dragon. Joey had to unlock the secrets of the Time Wizard, a card Yugi had given him, to win the duel. Joey succeeded and won Red-Eyes B. Dragon, which would become his most trusted card.

Joey Is Possessed by Marik

In the Battle City tournament, Marik Ishtar possessed Joey and forced him to battle Yugi in a deadly duel. Both duelists were chained to an anchor during the duel, and the loser would be plunged into the ocean's depths. Yugi acrificed himself and let Joey win. His heroic action broke Marik's mind ontrol over Joey, who awoke from Marik's spell just in time to save his iend.

Joey Is Chosen to Fight Dartz

oey battled Mai gain when she was vorking for Dartz. During that duel oey was transported to the Dominion f the Beasts. There e pulled a sword ut of a crystal tone, releasing an normous dragon, Hermos. In doing o, he became one f those chosen to ght Dartz—and ained the Claw of Hermos card.

JOEY'S MONSTERS

Joey's got some powerful monsters in his arsenal, including many dragons and warriors. But one of his favorites is the cute Time Wizard, a card Yugi gave him as a symbol of their friendship.

Alligator's Sword

Type: Beast

Using spiked armor for defense, Alligator's Sword slashes with his razor-sharp namesake.

Alligator's Sword Dragon

Type: Dragon

This battler's personal dragon gracefully carries him into combat!

Axe Raider

Type: Warrior

A slicing double-headed ax is this monster's weapon of choice.

B. Skull Dragon

Type: Dragon

B. Skull Dragon is a commanding fusion of Joey and Yugi's monsters, illustrating the power of their friendship.

JOEY'S MONSTERS

Battle Steer
Type: Beast-Warrior

No cowboy can tame this steer, which wields a wicked-looking lethal trident.

Battle Warrior
Type: Warrior

What is this tough fighter's weapon of choice? His bare hands!

Flame Swordsman
Type: Warrior

The power of fire fuels this swordsman's mighty weapon!

Did You Know?

Joey has always relied on Flame Swordsman to win duels. "As long as this guy's standing next to me, there's no way I could possibly lose!" Joey once said.

Garoozis
Type: Beast-Warrior

If his massive head doesn't scare you, his double-bladed battle ax will!

Gearfried the Iron Knight
Type: Beast-Warrior

Legend has it that an ancient Swordmaster was so frightened of his own power that he sealed himself away in armor. In this form, he is Gearfried the Iron Knight.

Gearfried the Swordmaster
Type: Warrior

If Gearfried is on the field, and Joey uses his Release Restraint card, Gearfried's true (and more powerful) form is revealed: Gearfried the Swordmaster.

JOEY'S MONSTERS

Gilford the Lightning

Type: Warrior

This knight in shining armor storms any dueling field with electric energy.

Hermos

Type: Dragon

Joey freed this protector of Atlantis from the Dominion of the Beasts. Hermos can combine monsters to transform into amazing weapons.

Legendary Guardian of Atlantis!

Jinzo

Type: Machine

Jinzo can destroy any traps that are laid before it.

Panther Warrior

Type: Beast-Warrior

This monster has the agility of a cat and a sword sharper than a panther's claws.

JOEY'S MONSTERS

Red-Eyes B. Dragon

Type: Dragon

Slashing claws, swiping tail, snapping jaws—all tools of the trade for this mighty dragon.

Red-Eyes Black Metal Dragon

Type: Machine

With a body made of gleaming black metal, this dragon is the metallic counterpart of Red-Eyes B. Dragon—and it is even more powerful.

Rocket Warrior

Type: Warrior

It may be tiny, but this warrior really blasts off when it flies into battle!

Swamp Battleguard

Type: Warrior

This monster uses its spiked club to bash and smash anything that moves.

JOEY'S MONSTERS

Swordsman of Landstar

Type: Warrior

Although a bit comical, this warrior displays some of the finest swordsmanship on the dueling field.

Thousand Dragon

Type: Dragon

It's hard to tell what's worse—this dragon's powerful claws or its toxic breath.

Tiger Axe

Type: Beast-Warrior

Another feline warrior, Tiger Axe slashes at opponents with raw power and wild fury!

Time Wizard

Type: Spellcaster

Every time Joey uses this card, he takes a chance. The Time Wizard spins the arm on his scepter, and something different will happen each time, depending on where it lands. Time Wizard has the power to age monsters—it made Baby Dragon evolve into Thousand Dragon and Yugi's Dark Magician evolve into Dark Sage.

TÉA GARDNER

Téa and Yugi have a strong bond—they've known each other since they were little kids. Téa is the biggest cheerleader of the group, always encouraging everyone to believe in themselves. Téa loves her friends and is willing to help them any way she can.

Did You Know?
Téa doesn't duel often, but when she does, she relies on Fairy-Type monsters and Yugi's Dark Magician Girl.

"No matter how dark things may get, the special bond I share with my friends will always find a way to shine through!"

—Téa

TÉA'S BIG MOMENTS

Téa Defeats Mai

When Yugi lost his Star Chips to Kaiba in the Duelist Kingdom tournament, he also lost his chance to save Grandpa. Téa faced Mai, a skilled duelist, to earn Star Chips for Yugi. Touched by Téa's determination and her friendship with Yugi, Mai purposely lost the battle. Téa gave Yugi her winning Star Chips, and Yugi regained his courage to battle after witnessing Téa's brave move.

A Chilling Battle

On the way to the Battle City tournament, a mysterious boy named Noah hijacked Yugi and his friends and had them face The Big Five. Téa battled Big 2, also known as Crump, in a chilling battle on top of an iceberg. With each life point that she lost, Téa became more and more engulfed in a block of ice! But she blazed her way to victory when she used her Dark Magician Girl—combined with Dark Magician summoned from Yugi's deck—to defeat Big 2 and his Nightmare Penguin.

TRISTAN TAYLOR

Tristan and Joey have been friends since they were kids. You'll often find him hanging out with Joey, Yugi, and Téa on their travels. Tristan doesn't duel much, but he's great at supporting his friends and cheering them on. And when his friends are in trouble, Tristan will do anything he can to protect them.

Did You Know?
Tristan has a crush on Joey's sister, Serenity.

TRISTAN'S BIG MOMENTS

Tristan Saves Mokuba

Tristan had just bravely rescued Mokuba from Pegasus's guards when Yami Bakura approached him. The evil ancient spirit was looking for a new body to inhabit, and he wanted Mokuba. "Hand him over this instant, or I'll dispatch you to the graveyard, too," Yami Bakura demanded. But Tristan didn't give in. He pushed past Yami Bakura and snatched his Millennium Necklace, tossing it away.

Tristan Monkeys Around

When Noah captured Yugi and his friends in his virtual world, the rules of reality didn't apply. The Big Five stole his body and put Tristan's mind in the body of a robot monkey. The only good thing about being trapped in a monkey's body? Serenity thought he was cute!

THE THREE FACES OF BAKURA

In the world of Yu-Gi-Oh!, there isn't a more complicated character than Bakura. Was he a friend? Rival duelist? Sworn enemy? The answer to all of those questions is YES!

Yugi first met **Bakura** at Domino High School. Bakura was a nice kid with a charming British accent, and Yugi, Téa, Joey, and Tristan thought of him as a friend. Soon, however, they noticed that a dark force seemed to be taking over Bakura.

That dark force was the spirit of an ancient Egyptian who shared Bakura's body—much like how the ancient Pharaoh shared Yugi's body. Bakura had the Millennium Ring, and the evil inside the Ring seemed to be taking over Bakura. When darkness took complete control of Bakura, he became **Yami Bakura**. And Yami Bakura had one goal: to gain control of all seven Millennium Items.

Yami Bakura brought Pharaoh back to ancient Egypt in an elaborate Shadow Game. There, Yami Bakura hoped to re-write the past. Five thousand years ago, he was **Bandit King Bakura**, a possessor of dark energies. As a boy, he watched Pharaoh's uncle, Aknadin, destroy his village so he could create the Millennium Items. He grew up with one goal: to overthrow Pharaoh and all his court.

Did You Know?

When Zorc was defeated, that wasn't the end of Bakura. The nice kid known to Yugi and his friends returned.

BAKURA'S BIG MOMENTS

Bakura Reveals His Dark Side

Yugi and his friends were shocked when their good friend Bakura brought them all to the Shadow Realm and challenged Yugi to a duel with a twist—he transformed Joey, Téa, and Tristan into their favorite monsters! Yugi used the power of the Millennium Puzzle to beat Yami Bakura at his own game, and their friend Bakura was back to normal. But not for long!

Yami Bakura Duels Yami Yugi

In the first battle of the Battle City finals, Yami Bakura dueled Yami Yugi. Pharaoh had a powerful Egyptian God Card in his deck—Slifer the Sky Dragon. Yami Bakura used Destiny Board, and he almost won the duel. But in the end, Yami Yugi was triumphant with Slifer the Sky Dragon.

'ami Bakura Hides His Soul

Vhen Yami Bakura battled Yami Marik in a Shadow Game in the Battle
:ity finals, he lost the duel and his Millennium Ring. Everyone thought
e had been banished to the Shadow Realm, but they were wrong. Yami
akura hid his soul in a piece of the Millennium Puzzle, so he was saved
'om the Shadow Realm—and free to continue with his sinister, secret
lans to plunge the world into darkness.

'ami Bakura Battles Yugi in Ancient Egypt

nowing that Yugi would bring Pharaoh the secret of his name,
ami Bakura challenged Yugi to a duel. While Zorc raged through
ncient Egypt causing destruction, Yami Bakura used his strategy
eliminate all but one of Yugi's cards. Even with the odds against
im, Yugi won the duel and brought Pharaoh his secret name.

BAKURA'S MONSTERS

Yami Bakura battles with nightmarish monsters with twisted, dark powers.

Necrofear

Type: Fiend

This dark and powerful monster will strike fear in the hearts of your opponents.

Diabound

When Bandit King Bakura was a boy, his village was destroyed in order to create the Millennium Items. The villagers' angry spirits created this unstoppable monster, and Bakura summoned it when he attempted to overthrow Pharaoh.

BAKURA'S MONSTERS

Doomcaliber Knight

Type: Zombie

Usually it's easy to outrun the undead—but not when they're like this zombie, who gallops across the battlefield on a horse as black as night.

The Earl of Demise

Type: Fiend

Like a creepy corpse on Halloween night, this monster floats across the field, lit by an eerie glow.

Earthbound Spirit

Type: Fiend

This monster lives in the ground, and boasts impressive defense points—but you probably won't use it to attack.

Gernia
Type: Zombie

This is not your typical zombie. Gernia is an undead monster with massive claws and a long tail.

Goblin Zombie
Type: Zombie

When this hideous undead creature attacks, you'll need a lively battle strategy to defend against it!

Headless Knight
Type: Fiend

He might not have eyes to see you with, but this knight knows exactly where to aim his silver sword.

Lady of Faith
Type: Spellcaster

Her moves are mysterious and therefore are known to take her opponents by surprise.

BAKURA'S MONSTERS

Zorc

Is Zorc the biggest, baddest monster of them all? He might be. He has been called the embodiment of darkness, from which all evil is formed. Ages ago, he emerged from the Shadow Realm.

In ancient times, Zorc was resurrected when Aknadin created the seven Millennium Items. Zorc terrorized Egypt, and Yami Bakura tried to bring him into the modern world, too. Yugi found himself in the ultimate battle of light versus darkness, and Yami Bakura revealed the shocking truth—Zorc had become a part of him!

"There is no creature that can overcome me. My power is infinite!"
— Zorc

Seven-Armed Fiend

Type: Fiend

With seven sharp-clawed arms, this monster doesn't need weapons to take down its foes!

Necro Mannequin

Type: Zombie

One look at this twisted terror made up of cobbled-together body parts, and you'll be sleeping with the lights on!

Man-Eater Bug

Type: Insect

You'll need more than a flyswatter to take down this carnivorous creature!

GRANDPA MUTO

Yugi calls him Grandpa, but his real name is Solomon Muto. He is owner of the local gaming shop. Grandpa knows a lot about Duel Monsters, and teaches Yugi and his friends about believing in the "heart of the cards."

Did You Know?

- Grandpa was a world traveler and tomb hunter as a young man.
- He looks a lot like Shimon, the advisor to the Pharaoh in ancient Egypt.

GRANDPA'S BIG MOMENTS

Grandpa Discovers the Millennium Puzzle

As a young adventurer, Grandpa Muto visited Egypt in search of Pharaoh's tomb. He hired two guides to help him navigate through the trap-riddled tomb. The guides were lost in the traps—but Grandpa was saved by the spirit of Pharaoh Atem, and found the Millennium Puzzle.

Grandpa Teaches Joey

When Joey was first learning to duel, he lost to Téa five times in a row! That's when he asked Grandpa Muto to help him become a better duelist. Grandpa didn't like Joey's laid-back attitude, but he didn't give up on Joey, and over time Joey became a better duelist.

Grandpa Muto Is Apdnarg Otum!

In the KC Grand Championship, a mysterious masked duelist named Apdnarg Otum appeared in the first match to battle Joey. The stranger somehow knew all of Joey's strategies! On top of that, Apdnarg Otum (Grandpa Muto spelled backward) almost beat Joey with his arsenal of ancient monsters—but Joey was victorious in the end.

"Seto and I are a team. I never turn my back on him!"

—Mokuba

SETO KAIBA

Seto Kaiba is the CEO of KaibaCorp, a multinational high-tech corporation. Pegasus may have invented the Duel Monsters game, but Kaiba invented the Duel Disk and the virtual reality duel system used by duelists all over the globe.

Kaiba is just as passionate about dueling as he is about running his company. Ruthless and ambitious, he has used his wealth and power to overcome all of his challengers. He wanted to be the world's greatest duelist, and he knew that only Yugi stood in his path.

Kaiba was Yugi's greatest rival. The two duelists have been through a lot together, and through it all, Kaiba learned about honor from Yugi and his friends.

Did You Know?

- Kaiba claims that his first words were "Neutron Blast Attack!"
- Kaiba is connected to Guardian Seto in ancient Egypt.

MOKUBA KAIBA

Seto Kaiba grew up in an orphanage with his little brother, Mokuba, and the two brothers developed a strong bond there. Kaiba loved and protected Mokuba, and Mokuba looked up to his older brother. Kaiba always does everything he can for Mokuba, and Mokuba can usually be found at his brother's side, cheering him on and supporting him.

KAIBA'S BIG MOMENTS

Kaiba Takes Control of KaibaCorp

As a young man, Seto Kaiba worked hard to invent his virtual duel system. His adopted father, Gozaburo Kaiba, wanted to use the system for waging war instead of dueling. To get revenge, Seto approached The Big Five to help stage a takeover of KaibaCorp. Seto succeeded—and then stripped The Big Five of their power at KaibaCorp so he could run the business on his own.

Kaiba Duels Grandpa

Eager to become the world's best duelist, Kaiba offered to pay Grandpa Muto a huge sum for his Blue-Eyes White Dragon card. But Grandpa refused. So Kaiba faced Grandpa Muto in a duel. Kaiba won Blue-Eyes White Dragon—and then tore it up so that no one could ever us it against him! It turned out that he already had three of his own

Champion vs. Creator

Pegasus trapped Mokuba's soul in a card, forcing Kaiba to duel in order to save his brother. It was a fierce battle between Kaiba and the creator of the Duel Monsters game. Pegasus used the Millennium Eye to predict Kaiba's moves, defeating Kaiba—and trapping his soul in a card, too.

Kaiba Learns His Destiny

When Egyptologist shizu Ishtar reached out to Kaiba, offering nim a card more powerful than Exodia, he was intrigued. Ishizu evealed that Kaiba was once a sorcerer n ancient Egypt. She old Kaiba about the existence of three rare Egyptian God Cards, two of which had been stolen. She gave him the hird, Obelisk the Tormentor, and tasked him with recovering the stolen cards. "After this moment, Kaiba, your life will never be the same," she said—and she was right.

The Battle City Finals

Kaiba designed the entire Battle City tournament in order to draw out Marik and the Rare Hunters. He was determined to win the Egyptian God Cards from them. So when Kaiba lost to Yugi, he was devastated. As Yugi put it, "Kaiba was fighting for all the wrong reasons. And in the end, it was his own anger and jealousy that did him in."

KAIBA'S MONSTERS

Seto Kaiba prides himself on collecting some of the most powerful monsters out there. He wants to be the best duelist in the world, and getting strong monsters is an important step in achieving that goal.

Battle Ox

Type: Beast-Warrior

This ox wields a mighty battle ax so it can smash and chop its way to victory!

Blade Knight

Type: Warrior

This knight in shining armor protects itself with a powerful shield and attacks with a sharp, curved blade.

Blue-Eyes Ultimate Dragon

Type: Dragon

What makes this dragon Ultimate? How about three heads, an armored body, and awesome attack points!

KAIBA'S MONSTERS

Blue-Eyes White Dragon

Type: Dragon

This monster attacks with incredible power, along with uncontrolled ferocity and aggressive dragon strikes!

Critias

Type: Dragon

Kaiba was chosen to release the third legendary dragon knight from the Dominion of the Beasts: Critias. Critias has the power to combine with traps in order to create amazing new dragons.

Legendary Guardian of Atlantis!

Hitotsu-Me Giant

Type: Beast-Warrior

That's right! It giant! It very strong! It smash other monsters to bits!

KAIBA'S MONSTERS

Judge Man

Type: Warrior

You don't want to be called into this judge's courtroom. He's not only the judge—if he thinks you're guilty of trying to beat him, he'll also act as executioner!

La Jinn the Mystical Genie of the Lamp

Type: Fiend

If you encounter this wicked genie on the battlefield, you'll wish you had some strong defense cards!

Rabid Horseman

Type: Beast-Warrior

This half-beast, half-warrior gallops into battle and slashes at its opponents with unbridled fury.

Obelisk the Tormentor

Type: Divine-Beast

With his massive muscles, King's Knight is more powerful than Queen's Knight and Jack's Knight.

Egyptian God Card!

KAIBA'S MONSTERS

Rude Kaiser

Type: Beast-Warrior

With plenty of armor for protection, Rude Kaiser hacks away with two large blades firmly mounted to its wrists.

Saggi the Dark Clown

Type: Spellcaster

You won't see this clown juggle. The only tricks it performs are ones of might, magic, and dark illusion!

Swordstalker

Type: Warrior

Wicked confidence shows on this creature's face as it steps onto the dueling field, wielding its razor-sharp sword.

Vorse Raider

Type: Beast-Warrior

Known for its relentless fighting style and double-bladed staff, Vorse Raider is not an opponent to be taken lightly.

KAIBA'S MONSTERS

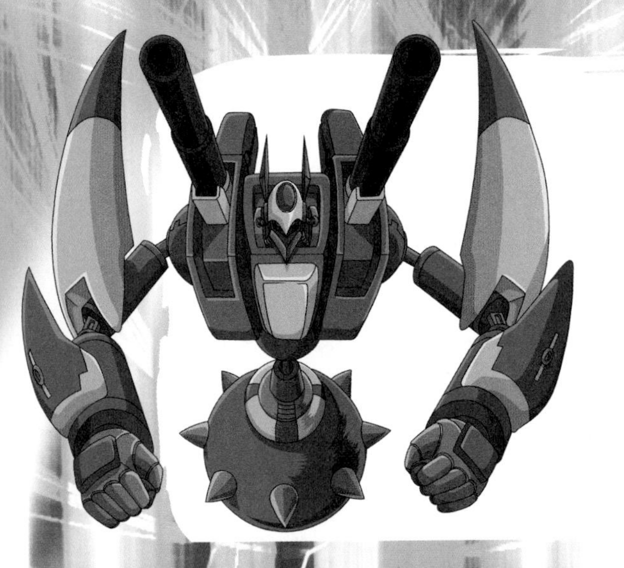

X-Head Cannon

Type: Machine

This mechanical monster can zip across the field, shooting powerful cannons at your opponents.

Y-Dragon Head

Type: Machine

This mechanical dragon pummels opponents with blasts of electric fire.

Z-Metal Tank

Type: Machine

This metal machine causes mayhem when it mows down everything in its path!

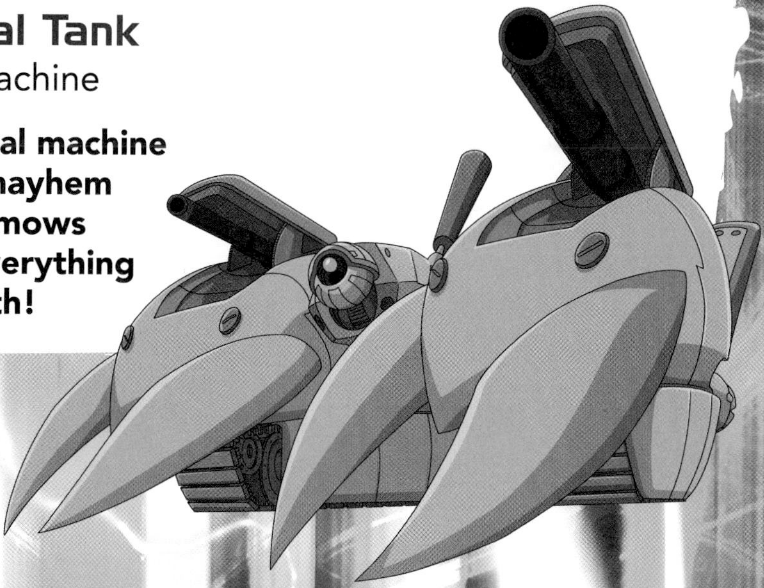

XYZ-Dragon Cannon

Type: Machine

What do you get when you combine X-Head Cannon, Y-Dragon Head, and Z-Metal Tank? A mammoth monster that unleashes massive mechanical mayhem!

MAI VALENTINE

Mai has got it going on, and she knows it! As one of the world's top duelists, she battles with skill, style, and flair. Some of her opponents get distracted by her good looks, but Mai doesn't mind—she uses that to her advantage.

Sometimes, Mai helps out Yugi and his friends. At other times, she is a dangerous opponent. It's difficult to predict what Mai will do, but one thing is for sure—she'll always be tough to beat in a duel!

Did You Know?
Mai is as comfortable on a motorcycle as she is on a dueling field.

"I do things my way and that's how I like it!"

—Mai

MAI'S BIG MOMENTS

Mai vs. Marik

In the third round of the Battle City finals, Mai was paired against Yami Marik in a Shadow Game. In a bold move, she took Marik's Egyptian God Card—The Winged Dragon of Ra. But Marik regained control of the beast, and turned the dragon's power against Mai. Marik sent Mai to the Shadow Realm—and she was changed forever.

Haunted by the Past

Haunted by her ime in the Shadow Realm, Mai tried to ill her loneliness by vinning duels—but ier victories only nade her feel more empty. So when the vil Dartz found Mai, e made her an offer he couldn't refuse—ltimate power in xchange for serving he Orichalcos. When hat evil card is played, it claims the loser's soul. It was a terrible bargain, ut Mai wanted to make sure she would never lose—and be sent back to he Shadow Realm—again.

MAI'S MONSTERS

Mai's collection of monsters reflects Mai's personality—they are all strong women!

Amazoness Chain Master

Type: Warrior

Amazons are some of the most powerful warriors in the world. This one extends her strikes with a long, spiked chain!

Amazoness Fighter

Type: Warrior

This warrior uses brute force to overpower her enemies.

Amazoness Swords Woman

Type: Warrior

A finely honed sword is the weapon of choice for this Amazon.

MAI'S MONSTERS

Harpie Lady

Type: Winged Beast

With the body of a woman and the claws and wings of a bird, Harpie Lady flies into battle with fierce intent. She is Mai's signature card—Mai never goes into battle without her.

Harpie Lady Sisters

Type: Winged Beast

These three sisters are very close—so close that they fight as one and leave opponents few choices for attack and defense!

Harpie's Pet Dragon

Type: Dragon

The only trick this pet does is battling opponents with its jagged claws and teeth.

MAXIMILLION PEGASUS

'he brilliant inventor of the Duel Monsters game, Pegasus vas admired by duelists everywhere. Then Yugi and his riends learned that Pegasus had a mysterious dark side. 'egasus's Millennium Eye gave him strange and magical owers, including the ability to duel in the Shadow Games, vhere monsters are real. As the creator of the game, Pega-us is also a master duelist with some of the most powerful nonster cards in existence in his arsenal.

Did You Know?
When Dartz was trying to destroy the world, Pegasus warned Yugi and gave him a card he could use to defeat Dartz.

CECELIA

'egasus first set eyes on the blonde-haired, blue-eyed Ce-celia when they were children. They got married as soon as hey were old enough, but shortly after the wedding Cecelia ell ill and died.

Distraught by the loss of his one true ove, Pegasus spent years trying to find a way to bring her back. He developed an elaborate plan to take over Kaiba-Corp and collect all the Millennium tems so he could bring Cecelia back o life.

PEGASUS'S BIG MOMENTS

Pegasus Receives the Millennium Eye and Creates Duel Monsters

As a young man, Pegasus was brokenhearted after the death of his young wife. He traveled to Egypt to search for the ancient secrets of reviving the dead. There he encountered Shadi, guardian of the Millennium Items. Shadi replaced Pegasus's left eye with the Millennium Eye and Pegasus learned of the ancient Shadow Games. When he returned to his company, Industrial Illusions, he created the Duel Monsters card game based on what he'd learned in Egypt.

Pegasus Steals Grandpa's Soul

After Pegasus beat Yugi in a Shadow Game, Pegasus kidnapped Grandpa Muto's soul. Then he forced Yugi to compete in the Duelist Kingdom tournament to save his grandfather.

Pegasus Loses to Yugi

After rounds of eliminations, Yugi and Pegasus faced off in the Duelist Kingdom final battle. There was a lot more at stake than a championship—Pegasus had captured the souls of Kaiba and Mokuba as well as Grandpa Muto.

Pegasus came to this Shadow Game with another advantage—with his Millennium Eye, he could read Yugi's mind, seeing in advance every move Yugi was going to make. But Joey, Tristan, and Téa blocked the Millennium Eye with the power of friendship, and Yugi defeated Pegasus to win the tournament—and the souls of Grandpa and his friends.

PEGASUS'S MONSTERS

As a kid, Pegasus loved to watch cartoons. His Toon World deck features lots of twisted toon monsters.

Blue-Eyes Toon Dragon

Type: Dragon

This dragon is small but strong and swift!

Dark Rabbit

Type: Beast

This may be one funny-looking bunny, but there's nothing funny about the way it attacks.

Dragon Piper

Type: Pyro

What magical spells might flow from this piper's flute?

Manga Ryu-Ran

Type: Dragon

Newly hatched, this "baby" dragon was born with plenty of power and giant stomping feet.

Parrot Dragon

Type: Dragon

When its beak snaps shut, this parrot tries to snatch more than just a tasty cracker!

PEGASUS'S MONSTERS

Relinquished
Type: Spellcaster

With its puzzling body, this creature keeps its opponent guessing about upcoming attacks.

Ryu-Ran
Type: Dragon

This young dragon is busting out of its shell! It was born with more strength than grown dragons.

Thousand-Eyes Restrict

Type: Spellcaster

Any opposing monster will feel weak at the knees when the endless eyes of this beast stare at it.

Toon Mermaid

Type: : Aqua

She may look cute and harmless, but watch out when she starts shooting her arrows—she's a great shot!

Toon Summoned Skull

Type: Fiend

Who knew that summoning Toons could be so powerful? You will, after your monsters face this creature.

THE TWO FACES OF MARIK

Marik Ishtar is Ishizu Ishtar's younger brother. For centuries, the Ishtar family was charged with protecting Pharaoh's tomb. They were not allowed to see the outside world.

Young Marik never wanted to be a tomb keeper, but his father forced him to become one. When Marik tried to explore the outside world, his father banished Odion, his adopted brother and best friend.

Rebellious evil rose inside Marik, and **Yami Marik** took over his body. Ishizu was always sure she could reach the good in her brother somehow, and Odion never failed to look after Marik. But Marik became obsessed with one goal: to obtain all three Egyptian God Cards and take Pharaoh's place.

Yami Marik put together a group of duelists called the Rare Hunters to help him find the cards by any means necessary. But while Yami Marik was busy being evil, part of the original Marik's spirit still lived, hoping to return to his body once more.

Did You Know?

When young Marik visited the outside world for the first time, he became obsessed with the idea of riding a motorcycle.

"There's nothing I like more than toying with someone's mind!"

—Yami Marik

YAMI MARIK'S BIG MOMENTS

Yami Marik Controls Joey's Mind

In his quest to get the Millennium Puzzle from Yugi, Yami Marik used his Millennium Rod to control the minds of Yugi's closest friends—Joey and Téa. Then he pitted Joey and Yugi in a duel by the sea—with the loser dumped into the ocean! Yami Marik ordered Joey to destroy Yugi, but the strength of Joey's bond with Yugi helped him break free.

Yami Marik vs. Bakura

In the Battle City finals, Yami Marik and Yami Bakura faced off with high stakes. The winner would gain the Millennium Rod and the Millennium Ring—and the loser would be trapped inside the Shadow Realm forever! Yami Bakura had help from an unexpected ally—the original spirit of Marik, who knew all of Yami Marik's battle moves. Yami Marik defeated Yami Bakura, certain that he had banished him to the Shadow Realm. Little did he know, Bakura had a trick up his sleeve. . .

Marik Gets His Body Back

In the Battle City finals, Yami Marik faced Yami Yugi in the final duel of the Battle City tournament. The power of The Winged Dragon of Ra nearly destroyed Yami Yugi and sent Yugi to the Shadow Realm. But before he could, Marik's adopted brother Odion showed up. He encouraged the original Marik to retake his body. Finding new strength, Marik overpowered Yami Marik and surrendered the duel to Yami Yugi. He apologized for failing Yugi, and repaid Pharaoh. He showed Yugi the secret tattooed on his back. This tattoo was the key to unlocking his memories. And he gave Yugi The Winged Dragon of Ra, as well as his two Millennium Items—the Millennium Rod and Millennium Ring.

MARIK'S MONSTERS

Marik's deck is filled with powerful monsters—but none are more powerful than his Egyptian God Card, The Winged Dragon of Ra.

Drillago

Type: Machine

This machine monster doesn't need fangs or claws—it has powerful spinning drill bits!

Juragedo

Type: Fiend

This freaky blue beast is full of surprises.

Lava Golem

Type: Fiend

This creature of living lava packs an astonishing three thousand attack points!

Legendary Fiend

Type: Fiend

With its blue muscled body, huge black wings, and fanged monster heads for hands, this monster's creepiness is legendary!

Lekunga

Type: Plant

It's alive! This creepy plant has one giant red eye that's always watching for a chance to attack.

MARIK'S MONSTERS

Lord Poison

Type: Plant

If its spiky thorns don't get you, its poison will!

Makyura the Destructor

Type: Warrior

Many warriors carry a sword, but Makyura is equipped with six sharp blades.

The Winged Dragon of Ra

Type: Divine-Beast

This is one of the three legendary and ultra-powerful Egyptian God Monsters. With this golden monster in your hand, you'll almost never lose. But will you be powerful enough to control it?

Egyptian God Card!

NOAH KAIBA

Noah is the son of Gozaburo Kaiba, the original founder of KaibaCorp. When he was ten years old he was in an accident, and his father uploaded his mind into a virtual world created for him on a supercomputer.

Poor Noah received no love or guidance in the virtual world, and years after his accident he trapped his adopted brother, Seto Kaiba, in there with him—along with Yugi and his friends. Noah forced them to battle The Big Five in hopes of winning a new body for himself. In the end, though, he proved that even the baddest villains have a soft spot.

Did You Know?

Gozaburo originally adopted Seto to use his body for Noah—and then decided he wanted to groom Seto to be his successor instead.

NOAH'S BIG MOMENTS

Noah Turns His Brothers into Stone

After Yugi's friends defeated The Big Five, Noah decided to battle his brother Seto himself in order to gain control of KaibaCorp. He used mind control on Mokuba, Seto's little brother and Noah's own adopted brother. Seto broke the mind control in time to win the duel. But in a virtual world, anything can happen...and Noah turned both his brothers into stone!

Noah Saves Yugi and His Friends

When Noah finally discovered a way to escape the virtual world, he took over Mokuba's body and escaped into the real world. He was poised to destroy the supercomputer and everyone trapped in it—including his brothers, Yugi, and Yugi's friends—but he changed his mind at the last minute. He left Mokuba's body and saved everyone in the virtual world, sacrificing himself in the process.

NOAH'S MONSTERS

The monsters Noah selects could all be characters in a twisted mythology.

Aeris

Type: Fairy

This powerful creature prefers fighting with weapons to fighting with spells.

Asura Priest

Type: Fairy

This godlike creature has many arms, which makes it a danger to all of the monsters on your opponent's side.

Gradius

Type: Machine

This high-performance jet fighter has several different attacks in its arsenal.

Hino-Kagu-Tsuchi

Type: Pyro

This fiery creature will make your opponents feel the burn!

Inaba White Rabbit

Type: Beast

This strange rabbit is nobody's pet. Send it hopping across the battlefield to hit your opponent's life points.

NOAH'S MONSTERS

Otohime

Type: Spellcaster

Spellcasting monsters like the beautiful Otohime may not pack attack power, but their spells can cause chaos for your opponents.

Shinato, King of a Higher Plane

Type: Fairy

This angelic-looking creature comes loaded with major attack and defense points.

Yamata Dragon

Type: Dragon

Noah used this seven-headed metal monster when he battled Yami Yugi.

Yata-Garasu

Type: Fiend

This purple crow returns ready to strike again.

DARTZ

This prince looks pretty good for ten thousand years old, doesn't he? Dartz was the son of the king of the legendary kingdom of Atlantis. After the kingdom fell, Dartz sought to resurrect the beast, Grand Dragon Leviathan, to destroy Earth so Atlantis could rise again.

To revive Grand Dragon Leviathan, Dartz fed it souls that he captured with The Seal of Orichalcos. But he believed that one soul was the key to his quest: the powerful soul of Pharaoh. When Pharaoh returned, Dartz sent his duelists to attack Yugi and his friends. Dartz never got Pharaoh's soul—so he used his own to bring Grand Dragon Leviathan back to life.

"Soon we shall rid the Earth of mankind, and rebuild civilization as it once was."

—Dartz

DARTZ'S BIG MOMENTS

Dartz Steals the Egyptian God Cards

"What kind of knucklehead would steal all three Egyptian God Cards, and then summon them right in the middle of the city for everyone to see?" Joey asked when the giant monsters arrived to terrorize the city. That would be Dartz, but he probably wouldn't like being called a knucklehead. He released the power of the cards to terrorize the modern world.

Dartz Resurrects Grand Dragon Leviathan

After ten thousand years, Dartz finally needed just one more powerful soul to revive the Grand Dragon Leviathan. He engaged Yami Yugi in a fierce battle. Pharaoh called upon the three legendary knights of Atlantis—Timaeus, Hermos, and Critias—and defeated Dartz. But Dartz wasn't finished with his plan. He sacrificed his own soul, and the great monster rose again.

DARTZ'S MONSTERS

Dartz uses every one of his monsters to achieve his ultimate goal: to resurrect the greatest monster of all, Grand Dragon Leviathan.

Divine Serpent Geh

Dartz called on this infinitely powerful card when he battled Yugi, but it was not able to deliver him to victory.

Grand Dragon Leviathan

A creature of pure evil, Leviathan is almost indestructible. It takes the combined power of all three legendary knights of Atlantis to bring it down.

Orichalcos Kyutora

What's creepy about a giant, spiderlike monster with a big human eye in its body? Everything!

MORE DUELISTS A-Z

Yugi and his friends have traveled around the world, making friends, battling enemies, and competing with other duelists. Meet some of the most memorable ones—and their monsters.

ALISTER

Alister is one of Dartz's henchmen. Since he was a boy, he has blamed KaibaCorp for his brother's death and was determined to seek revenge. He battled Kaiba on top of an airplane flying hundreds of miles an hour! He didn't care if the duel destroyed them both.

Alister's Major Monster

His **Air Fortress Ziggurat** is more than a monster—it's a flying mechanical fortress of destruction!

ARKANA

This former stage magician was one of Marik's Rare Hunters. He battles with the flair of a stage performer. In the Battle City tournament, he transported Yugi to a dangerous dueling arena where the loser would get sent to the Shadow Realm. Then Arkana pulled out a Dark Magician card to battle against Yugi's Dark Magician. Luckily, Yugi had a trick of his own up his sleeve. He called on Dark Magician Girl and won the duel.

Arkana's Major Monster

Arkana's **Dark Magician** looks different than Yugi's Dark Magician. He wears red and gold robes and appears older and more evil.

THE BIG FIVE

Trapped in a virtual world, Noah needed help with his plan to get revenge on his adopted brother, Seto, and get a new body. He turned to the former board of KaibaCorp—five ruthless businessmen known as The Big Five.

Big 1: Gansley

Gansley battled Yugi in the virtual world, where the dueling rules were different and far more complicated. But Yugi quickly got the hang of it and defeated Gansley.

Gansley's Major Monster

Gansley called on the underwater creature **Deepsea Warrior** when he battled Yugi, but he totally wiped out!

Big 2: Crump

Crump tried to freeze Téa in a battle on an iceberg field, but she blazed her way to victory.

Crump's Major Monster

You'd never find Crump's fiendish Nightmare Penguin in a zoo! But this aquatic monster couldn't defeat Téa.

Big 3: Johnson

Johnson cheated his way through his battle with Joey, but when Noah caught him, he made Johnson stop. Joey won the duel fair and square.

Johnson's Major Monster

A big bully, Judge Man controlled the outcome of Joey's moves... until Johnson got caught cheating.

Big 4: Nezbitt

Nezbitt challenged Duke, Tristan, and Serenity, hoping to be able to control all three of their bodies! But these three friends relied on teamwork to take down Big 4.

Nezbitt's Major Monster

Nezbitt calls on **Robotic Knight**, a machine monster and strict commander of other machines.

Big 5: Leichter

Noah saved Kaiba's former right-hand man for last, hoping to take down his adopted brother, Seto Kaiba. Leichter tried his best to annihilate Kaiba, but Blue-Eyes White Dragon helped give Kaiba the victory.

Leichter's Major Monster

Leichter's **Satellite Cannon** attacked Kaiba's monsters from deep space, where none of Kaiba's monsters could reach it!

BANDIT KEITH

Don't look for a fair match when you duel Bandit Keith. This bad guy will do anything he can to win—even if it means cheating! His deck is loaded with machine monsters.

Bandit Keith's Big Moment

Joey and Bandit Keith faced each other in the Duelist Kingdom Tournament. For most of the match, Bandit Keith's mechanical monsters blasted Joey's monsters off of the field. But Joey used his strategy to transform Red-Eyes B. Dragon into Red-Eyes Black Metal Dragon, making him strong enough to withstand Keith's assaults—and win the duel.

Bandit Keith's Major Monsters

Bandit Keith boasts a deck filled with powerful Machine monsters, including **Launcher Spider**, **Pendulum Machine**, and **Slot Machine**. When he joined the Rare Hunters, they beefed up his deck with a beastly monster, **Zera the Mant**.

Pendulum Machine

Launcher Spider

Slot Machine

BONZ

"Ahhhh! A ghost!" Joey cried when he first saw Bonz. This creepy kid is the smallest member of Bandit Keith's gang.

Bonz's Big Moment

Hoping to knock out the competition for Duelist Kingdom, Bandit Keith's gang kidnapped Joey and brought him to a creepy underground graveyard to duel Bonz. "Abandon hope, for no duelist gets out alive!" Bonz told Joey. His Zombie cards had an advantage on the graveyard field, but after some encouragement from Yugi, Joey buried Bonz's zombies and won the duel.

Bonz's Major Monsters

This duelist's deck is as spooky as he is, and it's loaded with Zombie monsters: **Armored Zombie**, **Clown Zombie**, **Crass Clown**, and **Pumpking the King of Ghosts**.

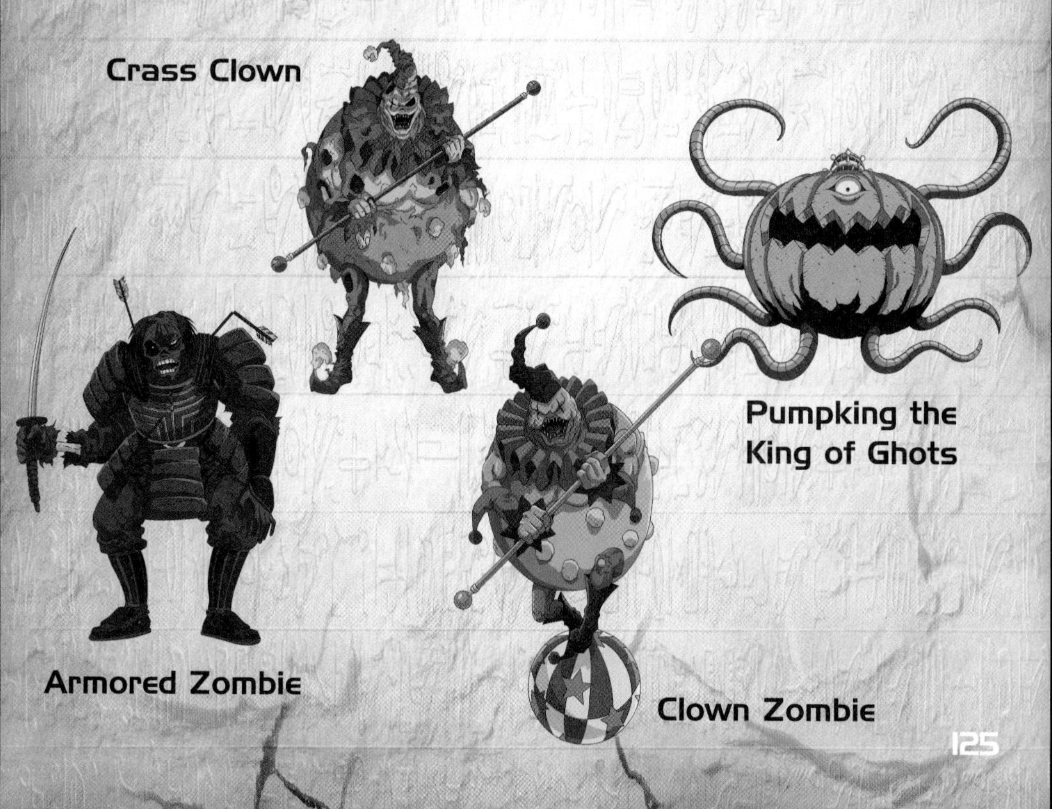

Crass Clown

Pumpking the King of Ghots

Armored Zombie

Clown Zombie

DUKE DEVLIN

Duke is the inventor of the Dungeon Dice Monsters game. He got off on the wrong foot with Yugi and his friends, and he and Joey often clash—probably because he beat Joey in a duel and then made him wear a dog costume when he lost. But Duke eventually became a good friend to the group, helping them out more than once when they got into trouble.

Duke's Major Monsters

Duke's deck holds some of the coolest Warrior monsters around. **Orgoth the Relentless** is an armored knight with powerful attack and defense points. And **Strike Ninja** moves like a shadow but attacks like a storm.

ESPA ROBA

Joey faced this duelist in the Battle City tournament. He claimed to have psychic powers, and at first Joey believed him. He knew every move Joey was going to make! Then Joey discovered that Espa Roba was using his younger brothers to spy on the cards in his hand. Joey recovered and sent the phony duelist packing.

Espa Roba's Major Monster

Espa Roba's Jinzo is a creepy Machine monster with a human brain. When he played it, Jinzo destroyed every trap in its way!

GOZABURO KAIBA

Gozaburo is the father of Noah, and the adopted father of Seto and Mokuba—and an overall bad guy. When he adopted Seto, he planned to give his body to Noah, whose spirit was trapped in a virtual world. When Seto invented a virtual reality system, he wanted to use it for entertainment purposes. But Gozaburo wanted to use it as a war machine. Seto responded by taking over KaibaCorp. Gozaburo returned later in the virtual world to battle his adopted son one last time. Seto beat Gozaburo, ending a painful chapter in his past forever.

Gozaburo's Major Monster

"Don't judge a monster by its cover. **Exodia Necross** is invincible!" Gozaburo boasted of this Spellcaster monster. But Kaiba found a way to defeat it.

GURIMO

Gurimo was a loyal follower of Dartz. He served his master by dueling Weevil Underwood and Rex Raptor and sealed their souls inside the Orichalcos. When Dartz's henchmen stole the three Egyptian God Cards from Yugi, Gurimo battled Yugi, using his own Obelisk the Tormentor against him. Yugi used strategy to defeat the powerful card, and Gurimo lost his soul to The Seal of Orichalcos. But he refused to give the God Cards back to Yugi.

Gurimo's Major Card

Gurimo was the first duelist to face Yugi using the sinister **The Seal of Orichalcos** card. The card allows the duelist to have ten monsters on the field at once, but its true power is more evil. The loser of the duel will have its soul absorbed by the Seal!

GUARDIANS OF THE PHARAOH

In ancient Egypt, Pharaoh Atem had six guardians. Each one possessed a Millennium Item.

Aknadin
Item: Millennium Eye

Aknadin was the brother of Pharaoh Aknamkanon. In an attempt to save his kingdom, he destroyed a village in order to make the Millennium Items. Before he carried out this terrible deed, he left behind his wife and son—Seto—to keep them safe.

Seto grew up knowing nothing of his royal heritage. When Bakura returned, darkness took over Aknadin. He vowed to overthrow Pharaoh so that his own son, Seto, could take the throne. When he tried to betray Pharaoh, Zorc rewarded him with powerful dark energies, transforming him into the Great Shadow Magus.

Isis
Item: Millennium Necklace

Isis is able to see the future with her necklace. During the battle with Zorc, she bravely attacked him, but she had already been weakened and was sent to the Shadow Realm.

Karim
Item: Millennium Scale

Karim was one of the six guardians of Pharaoh in ancient Egypt. He bravely battled Bakura and his Diabound monster, but was injured during the fight. Greatly weakened, he asked his friend, the guardian Shada, to take his remaining energy. "Before I enter the Shadow Realm, I want Pharaoh to have my strength," he said. His sacrifice allowed Shada to defeat one of Bakura's monsters, saving Pharaoh.

Mahad
Item: Millennium Ring

To protect Pharaoh, Mahad lured Bakura into a one-on-one duel. To battle Bakura's powerful Diabound, he called on his Illusion Magician. Unable to defeat Bakura, Mahad sacrificed himself to merge with Illusion Magician, becoming the Duel Monster known as Dark Magician.

Shada
Item: Millennium Key

This tattooed Egyptian was one of Pharaoh's strongest guardians. He saved Pharaoh from a lightning strike by Zorc and was cast into the Shadow Realm. "Know this, my friend. Your actions will not be in vain," Pharaoh promised him. "I will defeat this menace!"

Seto
Item: Millennium Rod

After Aknadin became the Great Shadow Magus, he begged Seto to join the dark forces with him and take his rightful place as Pharaoh. Seto was horrified by Aknadin's actions, especially when his father trapped the dragon spirit of his friend Kisara inside a stone tablet. Kisara's spirit became the Duel Monster known as Blue-Eyes White Dragon, and saved Seto from Aknadin. Seto is linked to modern-day Seto Kaiba.

ISHIZU ISHTAR

Since ancient times, the Ishtar family has guarded Pharaoh's secrets. Ishizu Ishtar grew up to work for the Egyptian Historical Society, where she studied the ancient dueling games.

Ishizu's study was aided by the Millennium Item she wore—the Millennium Necklace. It allowed her to view the future of the games. It was Ishizu who explained the connection between Yugi and Kaiba and the ancient Egyptians of the past.

Ishizu's Big Moment

When Ishizu brought her exhibit to the Domino Museum, she included a stone tablet that showed the ancient battle between Pharaoh and his Sorcerer. She showed the stone to Seto Kaiba, hoping that he would see the truth—Kaiba wasn't interested in Ishizu's story—until she told him about the three Egyptian God Cards and asked for his help in retrieving them.

Ishizu's Major Monsters

Ishizu doesn't duel often, but when she does, she uses powerful Fairy monsters that look like they were released from a Pharaoh's tomb: **Agido**, **Keldo**, **Mudora**, and Zolga.

JEAN CLAUDE MAGNUM

This duelist is also an actor who starred in ninja action movies. When he challenged Mai to a duel, he was hoping to earn a place in the Battle City finals. But he had a different goal in mind: to win Mai's hand in marriage! Jean Claude should have known better. Mai's warriors made mincemeat out of the actor's ninjas.

Jean-Claude's Major Monsters

This movie star's deck was stacked with ninja monsters, including **Ninja Master Shogun**.

JOHNNY STEPS

So you think you can duel? A dancing duelist might sound like fun, but Johnny Steps was a cheater who tried to trip up Téa when he challenged her to a dance battle. But Téa was fast on her feet and defeated this wannabe superstar.

Johnny's Major Monsters

Johnny's deck holds musical monsters like **Spirit of the Harp**. When he used fusion to combine **Witch of the Black Forest** and **Lady of Faith**, he created **Musician King**, who plays a mean guitar.

LEON VON SCHROEDER

Leon has grown up under the shadow of his older brother, the famous duelist Zigfried von Schroeder. Leon dreamed of facing Yugi ever since he saw Yugi compete in the Duel Monsters tournament, and he finally got his chance in the Grand Championship.

When Kaiba defeated Zigfried, he was disqualified from the tournament. Zigfried convinced Leon to help him get revenge. When Leon was dueling with Yugi, Zigfried asked him to use a card containing a virus that would destroy KaibaCorp. Leon agreed at first, but then he tried to stop the virus. He asked Yugi for help and together they saved the game before it was too late.

Leon's Major Monsters

Leon is obsessed with fairy tales and uses storybook monsters such as **Hexe Trude**, **Globerman**, and **Little Red Riding Hood**.

LUMIS AND UMBRA

This masked team of duelists were part of Marik's Rare Hunters. They forced Kaiba and Yugi into a tag-team duel with huge stakes: the losers would plummet from the top of a skyscraper into the Shadow Realm! Their practiced teamwork nearly beat Kaiba and Yugi, who were having a tough time working together. But in the end, Yugi and Kaiba worked through their differences and were able to defeat the masked duelists.

Luma and Umbra's Major Monster

This tag-team almost took down Yugi and Kaiba with **Masked Beast Des Gardius**, a terrifying Fiend monster with 3,300 attack points.

MAKO TSUNAMI

Joey faced off against Mako and his underwater monsters during the Battle City tournament, with a place in the finals on the line. A fisherman by trade, Mako dueled with honor.

Mako's Major Monster

Mako's favorite card was **The Legendary Fisherman**, a shark-riding warrior with wild hair. When Joey won the duel, Mako honored him by giving him this card.

MANA

In ancient Egypt, Mana grew up with Pharaoh, becoming his best friend. While Atem was destined to rule, Mana trained to become a spellcaster with the great magician Mahad. After Mahad transformed into Dark Magician, Mana vowed to protect her friend, Pharaoh.

Mana's Major Monster

When Yugi and his friends arrived in ancient Egypt, Mana was one of the first people they met. Yugi told Mana she looked like **Dark Magician Girl**, and Dark Magician Girl turned out to be her spirit monster.

ODION

Adopted into the Ishtar family, Odion is extremely loyal to his adoptive brother, Marik, and sister, Ishizu. Odion wants nothing more than to become a keeper of Pharaoh's tomb, but because he was not born an Ishtar he will never have that duty.

Odion's Big Moment

Odion was so loyal to Marik that when Marik asked him to become one of his Rare Hunters, he agreed. He even pretended to be Marik to trick Yugi and his friends. Odion, disguised as Marik, battled Joey in the second round of the Battle City tournament. But his deception was revealed when he played a phony version of the Egyptian God Card, The Winged Dragon of Ra. The Egyptian Gods were insulted, and they punished Odion. He lost the duel, and Yugi and his friends learned the true identity of Marik.

Odion's Major Monster

Mystical Beast Serket is a giant scorpionlike creature like something out of a nightmare!

PANIK

PaniK is a mean duelist who looks scarier than many Duel Monsters. He wears two large Duel Gloves to show he means business. In the Duelist Kingdom tournament, Pegasus hired him to take down duelists that he wanted out of the way. He dueled Mai and cheated her out of all of her Star Chips so that she couldn't proceed in the tournament. But Yami Yugi took on the big bully and won them back.

PaniK's Major Monster

You won't find a princess living in **Castle of Dark Illusions**. This dark fortress provides PaniK with a powerful defense by creating a dark mist that hides his monsters in the shadows.

PARADOX BROTHERS

Maximillion Pegasus hired these tough-looking twins to eliminate weak duelists from his Duelist Kingdom tournament. Yugi and Joey battled Para and Dox in an underground labyrinth. In order to beat the brothers and their powerful monsters, Yugi and Joey had to unleash the greatest power of them all—teamwork!

The Brothers' Major Monsters

In the battle against Yugi and Joey, the twins relied on **Shadow Ghoul**, a Zombie monster with endless red eyes. But their **Gate Guardian**, an enormous Warrior monster, gave the boys their biggest fight.

PROFESSOR ARTHUR HAWKINS

Professor Hawkins is the best friend of Yugi's grandfather, Solomon Muto. The two men met while exploring Egypt. Years later, when Dartz and his gang appeared, the professor researched the history of Atlantis and helped Yugi and his friends find Dartz's lair. He is the grandfather of duelist Rebecca Hawkins.

Arthur's Major Monster

When he was younger, he possessed a **Blue-Eyes White Dragon**, which he gave to Grandpa Muto.

REBECCA HAWKINS

This young duelist also happens to be a tournament champion. Convinced that Grandpa Muto stole Blue-Eyes White Dragon from her grandfather, Arthur Hawkins, she challenged him to a duel. Yugi dueled in his grandfather's place, and he surrendered the duel to Rebecca in order to teach her that there's more to dueling than winning and losing. (And she didn't get the card—it had already been destroyed!) Rebecca realized she had feelings for Yugi, and she joined him in the fight against Dartz.

Rebecca's Major Monsters

Rebecca uses a wide variety of cards and monsters, like **Fire Princess**. Her ability to master many different cards and monsters is a big part of what makes her a champion.

RAFAEL

This menacing, muscled duelist was Dartz's main henchman. Dartz convinced him that Pharaoh was evil, so he challenged Yugi to a Death Valley duel. Yami Yugi took over and took The Seal of Orichalcos from Rafael—and then used the sinister card. Rafael won the duel, and Yugi's soul was taken. In the end, Rafael realized that Dartz was wrong and tried to help Yugi defeat him.

Rafael's Major Monsters

Rafael relies on Guardian monsters: **Guardian Eatos**, **Guardian Grarl**, **Guardian Kay'est**, and **Guardian Dreadscythe**.

REX RAPTOR

Rex uses his dinosaur-loaded deck to overwhelm his opponents. But his big monsters make him overconfident. When he battled Weevil Underwood in Pegasus's regional championships, he thought his dinos would squash Weevil's bugs. But Weevil's strategy sent his dinosaurs to the graveyard.

Rex's Major Monsters

Rex might act funny sometimes, but his monsters are nothing to laugh it. His **Two-Headed King Rex** stomps all over his opponents.

SHADI

Shadi was the guardian of the seven Millennium Items. He believed that each Item was waiting for the person destined to possess it. When Maximillion Pegasus wandered into the Egyptian desert, Shadi gave him the Millennium Eye.

When Bakura stole the Millennium Eye from Pegasus, Shadi sensed that the cosmic balance had been upset, and he decided to investigate.

Shadi's Big Moment

When Pharaoh returned to ancient Egypt to recover his lost memories, it was Shadi who helped Yugi and his friends go back in time to find him. If not for Shadi, the world might have plunged into darkness forever.

STRINGS

With his bald head and big spooky eyes, Strings can make people feel uneasy—especially because he never speaks. He is known as The Quiet One. Since Strings is one of Marik's Rare Hunters, Marik made him to take down Yugi—and gave him Slifer the Sky Dragon to make sure he could seal the deal. But Yugi prevailed and got his card back when Strings lost the duel.

Strings' Major Monster

Strings revolved his strategy around the Egyptian God Card given to him by Marik—**Slifer the Sky Dragon**. But even with that powerful card, he couldn't defeat Yugi.

VALON

Valon was a troubled kid Dartz tricked into stealing souls. Valon recruited Mai to join Dartz's team, but his feelings for Mai are what eventually led to his downfall. Knowing how much Mai had once cared for Joey, Valon faced Joey in a battle with both of their souls at stake. Joey took a risk and turned Valon's strategy against him, and Valon lost his soul to The Seal of Orichalcos. Before he was taken, his last words were, "Wheeler, it's up to you now. Save Mai."

Valon's Major Monsters

Valon plays with Armor cards that give him special powers on the field.

VIVIAN WONG

Actress. Model. Kung fu Champion. Master Duelist. Yugi's Biggest Fan. Vivian Wong is all of these things and more. She defeated countless opponents to earn her place in the Grand Championship.

Once there, she faced the young duelist Rebecca Hawkins. Her Dragon Lady nearly destroyed Rebecca, but then Rebecca fought back with a combination of Guardian Angel Joan and Fire Princess to win the duel.

Vivian's Major Monster

One of Vivian's favorite cards is **Dragon Lady**, a Warrior who wields two sharp swords. Dragon Lady is strong on both attack and defense.

WEEVIL UNDERWOOD

Weevil is a competitive duelist and a great strategist. He competed in the Duelist Kingdom Tournament against Yugi and his friends. On the way to Duelist Kingdom, Weevil thought he could beat Yugi by throwing his best cards overboard, but Yugi sent him packing in the first round. You can usually find Weevil hanging out with duelist Rex Raptor.

Weevil's Major Monsters

Weevil favors a creepy, crawly deck of Insect monsters, including **Great Moth**, **Insect Queen**, and **Perfectly Ultimate Great Moth**.

Insect Queen

Great Moth

ZIGFRIED VON SCHROEDER

This purple-haired duelist had a beef with Kaiba. He believed that KaibaCorp stole technology from his company, Schroeder Corp. To get revenge, he entered the Grand Championship under the name Zigfried Lloyd. He defeated Joey, but then Kaiba defeated him.

Zigfried's Major Monster

Leading the charge against Zigfried's opponents are his Valkyrie monsters—battlers who ride majestic horses.

THE END?

Sure, Zorc has been defeated. Pharaoh has reunited with his friends in the afterlife. Does that mean that Yugi's adventures are over? Of course not!

Yugi, Joey, Téa, and Tristan are embarking on a new adventure. They'll battle new duels. Discover new Duel Monsters. Fight a new threat to the world.

And, like they always do, they'll do it together.

SPIRIT